Ferida Wolff

THE WOODCUTTER'S COAT

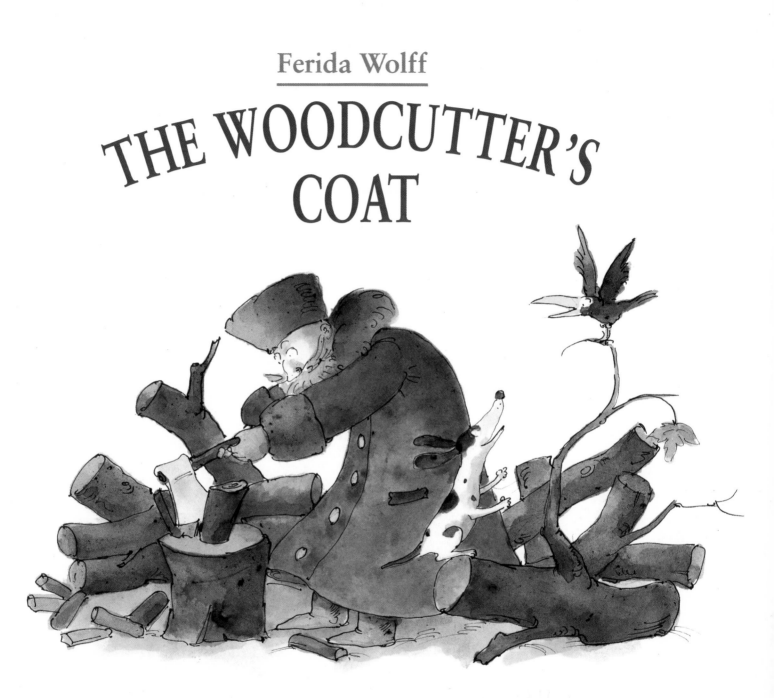

Illustrated by **Anne Wilsdorf**

Little, Brown and Company

Boston   Toronto   London

For Jeanne and Anna Marie
F. W.

First Edition

Library of Congress Cataloging-in-Publication Data

Wolff, Ferida, 1946–
    The woodcutter's coat / Ferida Wolff ; illustrated by Anne
Wilsdorf. — 1st ed.
        p.   cm.
    Summary: A woodcutter's coat is stolen, then passed from one
person to another until it comes back full circle to the woodcutter
himself.
    ISBN 0-316-95048-3
    [1. Coats — Fiction.]   I. Wilsdorf, Anne, ill.   II. Title.
PZ7.W82124Wo   1992
[E]—dc20   90-26635

Joy Street Books are published by
Little, Brown and Company (Inc.)

10 9 8 7 6 5 4 3 2 1

BER

Published simultaneously in Canada
by Little, Brown & Company (Canada) Limited

Printed in the United States of America

Once there was a woodcutter who lived at the edge of
the cold North Woods. He made his living by chopping
wood for the townspeople.

With the money he earned, he bought potatoes and eggs. He bought a stone to sharpen his ax. And he bought a fine, heavy coat with a thick fur collar and five round buttons to keep him warm while he worked.

Each morning, after eating his breakfast of eggs and potatoes, the woodcutter put on the fine coat, sharpened his ax, and went to work chopping wood.

The wind came in hard from the north, but the woodcutter was warm in his fine coat. He could work all day and not feel the cold. He chopped great piles of wood to sell in town.

As time passed, the coat no longer looked quite so fine. There was a stain on the pocket, and the fur lost its shine. The hem came loose and dragged on the ground. And as mighty blow followed mighty blow, one button after another popped off the coat until there were no buttons left.

"I should sew on some buttons," said the woodcutter. But somehow he never did.

Each time the woodcutter raised his ax, the coat flapped open, letting in the chill wind. The woodcutter shivered.

"What good is a coat if it doesn't keep you warm?" he said. "Tomorrow I will deliver this wood to the tailor and have him repair my coat while I'm in town."

In the morning, the woodcutter put on his coat, loaded the
wood into his wagon, and started down the road.

On the way he was stopped by a thief.

"Give me your money," the thief demanded.

"But I have no money!" said the woodcutter. "I have only this load of wood that I am bringing to the tailor."

The north wind blew. It chilled the thief through his old, worn coat.

"I don't need any wood," chattered the thief, "but I will take that fine coat you are wearing."

He put on the fine coat and tossed his own tattered coat to the woodcutter.

As the thief ran down the road toward town, the woodcutter's coat blew open and the icy wind made him shiver.

"Bah!" said the thief. "Some fine coat. It won't stay closed. I am just as cold as I was before. I must find another coat."

In town, the thief came upon a busy barbershop. He peeked in and saw a large man take off his handsome new coat, hang it on a hook by the front door, then sit down to get a haircut. The thief crept in and took the man's coat, leaving the woodcutter's coat on the hook instead.

When the man reached for his coat, all he found was the woodcutter's coat hanging on the hook.

Who could have taken my coat? he wondered. At least he left this fine one in its place. That is, it will be fine when I clean away this spot on the pocket.

He cleaned off the spot, put on the coat, and went outside.

The north wind swirled around him. The man tried to pull the
coat closed, but it would not fit over his large, round stomach.
"This will not do, not do at all," he said.

He went into the bakery to get out of the wind and complained to the baker about the woodcutter's coat.

"That looks like a fine coat," said the baker. "It just needs a few buttons. I will trade my cape for your coat."

The man left the bakery with six sticky buns and the baker's cape.

When his morning's work was finished, the baker sewed some buttons on the woodcutter's coat.

Then he started to load his delivery wagon with
the pies and cakes he had made. As he worked, the coat
tugged at his arms and pulled at his back. It began
to feel heavier and heavier.

"My cape was never this heavy," the baker grumbled.

The postman, stopping by with the day's mail, heard the baker groaning.

"What's wrong?" he asked.

"This heavy coat makes my work harder," said the baker.

"Hmmm," said the postman. "I am outside all day. I could use a
heavy coat to keep me warm. I will give you my lighter coat
if you will give me your heavier one."

The baker handed the coat to the postman. The postman felt the weight of the woodcutter's coat on his back.

"Ah," he said. "The wind won't get through this coat. But I see that the hem is coming down. I must fix it so that I don't trip as I walk."

The postman sewed the hem and went on delivering the mail.
The north wind blew. "It certainly is cold today," he said. He
pulled the collar of the coat up to his chin. The fur tickled his nose.

"Kitchoo, kitchoo, *kitchoo*," he sneezed. I must be getting sick, the postman thought. I'll stop to see the doctor when I deliver the mail.

"It is the fur that's making you sneeze," the doctor said. "You need a coat without a fur collar."

"But I gave my coat to the baker!" said the postman.

"That is a fine coat you are wearing," said the doctor. "My husband is looking for a coat just like that. Wait here. I will take your coat for my husband and give you his coat in return."

When the doctor's husband tried on the woodcutter's coat, he discovered that the sleeves were far too short.

"This is a fine coat," he said, "but it does not fit! I will have to go to the store and buy a new coat."

On his way out, he tossed the woodcutter's coat into
the trashbin.

A beggar found the coat and picked it up. It was dusty. The fur collar was matted down.

"It needs a little cleaning up," said the beggar, "but I can see that this is a fine coat. I can sell it for a good price."

The beggar brushed off the coat and fluffed up the fur until it was thick and shiny again. Then he took the coat to the tailor.

"This *is* a fine coat," said the tailor. "I will buy it from you."

"Yes, sir," he said when the beggar had left. "I can sell this fine coat. But first I will sew on a bit of trim to make it a little fancier."

Just as the tailor finished the last stitch, he heard a knock. It was the woodcutter bringing his winter supply of wood.

"Oh, dear," said the tailor. "I just bought this coat and have no money to pay you."

The tailor saw that the woodcutter's coat was tattered and old.

"Will you take this fine, warm coat instead?" he asked.

The woodcutter looked at the coat. It reminded him of the coat he used to have, except that the pockets were clean, the hem wasn't dangling, and the fur was nice and fluffy. It even had fancy trim. Best of all, this coat had five shiny buttons where his other coat had had no buttons at all.

"Well," said the woodcutter, "I do need a coat. . . ."

The woodcutter put on the fine coat with the thick fur collar and five shiny buttons.

"Why, I can work all day in this coat and not feel cold!" he said happily.

He started back to his cabin at the edge of the cold North Woods. As he waved good-bye to the tailor, a button popped off the coat. The woodcutter picked it up and put it in his pocket.

"I should sew on this button," he said.

But somehow, he never did.